# Immigration
## Starting a New Life

## Lisa Perlman Greathouse

**Image Credits:** Cover, p. 1 The Granger
Collection, New York / The Granger Collection;
7–24 Bridgeman Art Library; p. 3 North Wind
Picture Archives; all other images Shutterstock.

**Teacher Created Materials**
5301 Oceanus Drive
Huntington Beach, CA 92649-1030
http://www.tcmpub.com
**ISBN 978-1-4807-4456-1**

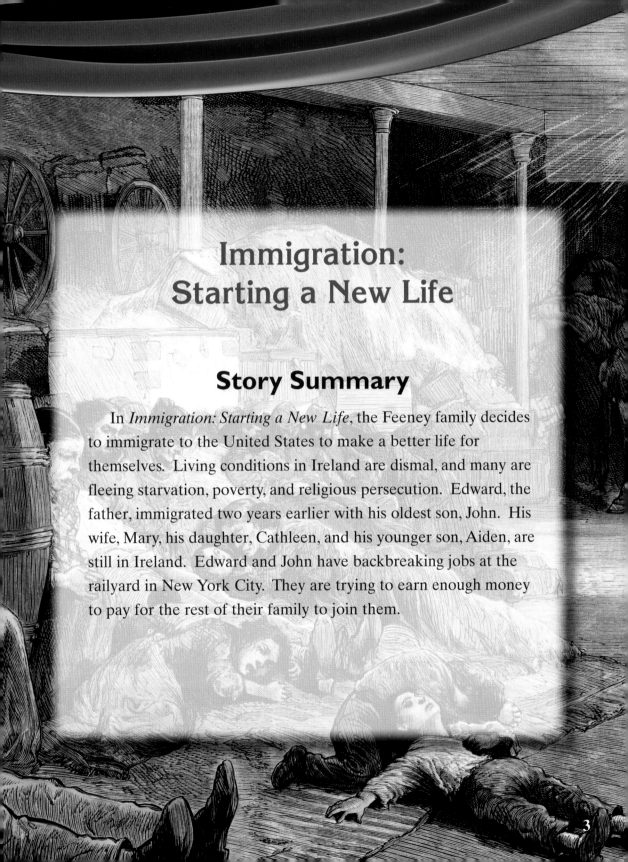

# Immigration: Starting a New Life

## Story Summary

In *Immigration: Starting a New Life*, the Feeney family decides to immigrate to the United States to make a better life for themselves. Living conditions in Ireland are dismal, and many are fleeing starvation, poverty, and religious persecution. Edward, the father, immigrated two years earlier with his oldest son, John. His wife, Mary, his daughter, Cathleen, and his younger son, Aiden, are still in Ireland. Edward and John have backbreaking jobs at the railyard in New York City. They are trying to earn enough money to pay for the rest of their family to join them.

# Tips for Performing Reader's Theater

## Adapted from Aaron Shepard

★ Don't let your script hide your face. If you can't see the audience, your script is too high.

★ Look up often when you speak. Don't just look at your script.

★ Talk slowly so the audience knows what you are saying.

★ Talk loudly so everyone can hear you.

★ Talk with feelings. If the character is sad, let your voice be sad. If the character is surprised, let your voice be surprised.

★ Stand up straight. Keep your hands and feet still.

# Tips for Performing
# Reader's Theater *(cont.)*

★ Remember that even when you are not talking, you are still your character.

★ If the audience laughs, wait for them to stop before you speak again.

★ If someone in the audience talks, don't pay attention.

★ If someone walks into the room, don't pay attention.

★ If you make a mistake, pretend it was right.

★ If you drop something, try to leave it where it is until the audience is looking somewhere else.

★ If a reader forgets to read his or her part, see if you can read the part instead, make something up, or just skip over it. Don't whisper to the reader!

# Immigration:
# Starting a New Life

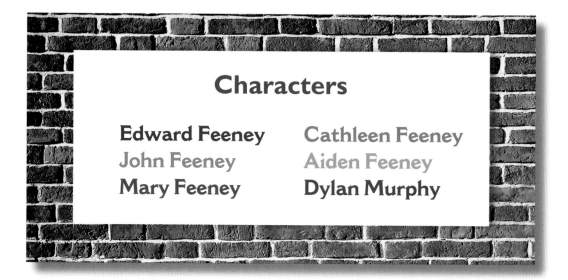

## Characters

| | |
|---|---|
| **Edward Feeney** | Cathleen Feeney |
| John Feeney | Aiden Feeney |
| **Mary Feeney** | **Dylan Murphy** |

## Setting

This reader's theater begins in February 1894. Mary, Cathleen, and Aiden are in Waterford, Ireland, waiting. Meanwhile, Edward and John are in New York City.

## Act I

| | |
|---|---|
| **Mary:** | Cathleen, a letter has finally arrived from your father! |
| **Cathleen:** | What are you waiting for Mother? What does Father's letter say—is his news optimistic? Are we finally going to travel to America to unite with Father and Johnny? |
| **Mary:** | Slow down, dear, so that I can read the letter aloud. |

*Dearest Mary,*

*Oh, how I miss you and the children so much. Johnny and I have been working hard at the railyard, and we have practically earned enough money to purchase the tickets for you, Cathleen, and little Aiden to join us. I should be able to prepay for your tickets in the next several weeks so that you and the children can be on the April 12 voyage. I understand that the steamships now dock at the immigration station in New York Harbor, called Ellis Island. Future correspondence should have all of the information. Oh, how I look forward to the day we will be reunited!*

*With much love to you and the children,*

*Edward*

| | |
|---|---|
| **Cathleen:** | April is only two months away! We should really begin preparing and packing for the voyage, Mother! How many of our belongings do you imagine we'll be allowed to bring on the ship? |

**Mary:** Cathleen, you know that this isn't the first time your father has hoped to buy the tickets for our trip. Last time, work slowed down and he didn't have enough money to buy all three, and we are certainly not going to travel to a new country one at a time.

**Aiden:** Did I hear that we are finally going to see Father and Johnny? I dreamt last night that we were all together again and that we lived in a big house in America.

## Poem: I Am the Little Irish Boy

**Aiden:** It's been so long since we've seen them that I can't really remember what they look like, and I have to look at their pictures to remind myself. For two years now, I keep hearing that we'll be going to America soon, but then the plans change. I can hardly believe that we'll finally see them again!

**Mary:** We aren't going anywhere just yet, Aiden. We will be joining your father and brother again, but we can't be positive exactly when.

**Cathleen:** The letter from Father says that we're going to America in a couple of months, Aiden! We will be traveling on a huge steamship, like in the photographs I showed you. We'll be landing in New York Harbor at an immigration station called *Ellis Island*. We will finally be reunited with Father and Johnny.

**Aiden:** I can't wait to arrive in America! Will we be allowed to go to school in the United States? Do you imagine they will allow our family to attend whichever church we choose?

**Cathleen:** Of course, silly brother! And we'll no longer share a bed or feel hungry at bedtime. There will be beef, fruit, vegetables, potatoes, and even sweets for dinner, and every single day will be like Christmas! People say that the streets in America are paved with the gold of opportunity. I cannot wait to leave Ireland behind with all its misery and hardships.

**Aiden:** I wonder if I'll be able to quickly make friends in America. Maybe I'll even manage to make friends on the voyage! Do you think I'll be allowed to bring my picture books, puzzles, and sketchpad with me on the trip?

**Mary:** Cathleen and Aiden, I can barely concentrate with you two jabbering on. Yes, Aiden, when we go, eventually, I'm certain you'll make friends and that you'll be allowed to take your belongings to America. Now, why don't you both entertain yourselves outside until supper is ready? And see who's at the door on your way out.

**Dylan:** Good afternoon, Mrs. Feeney. I was wondering if Cathleen is available for a visit.

**Mary:** Simply wonderful to see you, Dylan! I hope your family is healthy and doing well.

**Dylan:** Actually, Mrs. Feeney, Father has a high fever. Mother and I have been caring for him. The doctor is having a tough time discovering what is causing the fever, so he can't suggest a proper treatment for him. His condition seemed to be improving this afternoon, so Mother suggested I go out awhile and visit with friends.

| | |
|---|---|
| **Mary:** | Well, I'm certainly glad to hear he's recuperating. If you would like to visit with Cathleen, she's on her way outside to entertain Aiden. |
| **Dylan:** | Thank you very much for your gracious hospitality, Mrs. Feeney. I'm hoping to say hello to Cathleen, but I won't be staying long. |
| Aiden: | Look, Cathleen, your love-struck boyfriend's here! |
| Cathleen: | *(irritated)* Don't be ridiculous, little Aiden! *(coyly)* Dylan Murphy, you haven't visited in ages. How have you and your family been getting along? |
| **Dylan:** | Father hasn't been feeling well, lately. I desperately needed a break from caring for him, so I decided to visit you and your family. |
| Cathleen: | I'm so sorry to hear about your troubles, Dylan, but I'm happy you stopped by for a visit. |
| Aiden: | Cathleen, tell Dylan the exciting news! |
| Cathleen: | It looks as though Father is finally going to buy tickets for Mother, Aiden, and me to sail to New York City. I can hardly believe we'll be starting our new lives in America in just two months! |
| **Dylan:** | *(glumly)* That's magnificent news, Cathleen. |
| Cathleen: | Forgive me, Dylan, but you certainly don't appear to be very happy. |
| **Dylan:** | I am, sincerely, although I must admit, I'm going to miss you and your family terribly, Cathleen. We've been friends and classmates since we were . . . well, for as long as I can remember. |

| Aiden: | Not to mention that you're in love with each other. |
| --- | --- |
| Cathleen: | *(embarrassed)* Ignore him, Dylan. Honestly, Aiden, why don't you find someplace else—anywhere else—to play? You are utterly annoying sometimes! |

**Act 2**

| Edward: | Johnny, wake up immediately! It is imperative that we arrive at the railyard within 45 minutes. Mr. Nicholas won't hesitate to send you home penniless if you're tardy even two minutes. Also, allow for enough time to eat the oatmeal I've prepared for breakfast—an empty stomach won't help you work all day. |
| --- | --- |
| John: | Oatmeal again, Father? Can't I grab a biscuit at the railyard? I believe we can spare an extra minute; I really don't think Mr. Jenkins is likely to send me home without pay. He knows and appreciates that I work harder than just about anyone else at the railyard. Didn't you see the amount of lumber I moved yesterday? |
| Edward: | I don't appreciate your lazy attitude, young man. We don't want to take any chances when it comes to earning enough money to afford the voyage for your mother, sister, and brother. |
| John: | I'm sorry, Father; I'm just exhausted after working 16 hours yesterday and the day before that. I know conditions were terrible back in Ireland. I just never thought it would be so difficult to make a living here in America. |

| | |
|---|---|
| **Edward:** | The conditions are far worse than you know, Son. The potato famine left Ireland hopeless, with no employment prospects—only starvation and illness, even after all these years. Settling in America was our only hope for survival. |
| **John:** | I know, it's just that I'd be so much happier with a different job. |
| **Edward:** | You should be happy you have any employment. There are many immigrants just like us who haven't been fortunate enough to find any work. I guarantee our backbreaking efforts will be worth it when we are reunited with your mother and siblings. |
| **John:** | And if we get paid, like we're supposed to next month, maybe we will be together again by the end of April. |
| **Edward:** | After the numerous months apart, that would, indeed, be an answer to my prayers. I'll wager that little Aiden has grown so big we will hardly even recognize him. |
| **John:** | It's been so long that sometimes I'm afraid I've forgotten what Mother looks like. I have to look at her photograph to remind myself. |
| **Edward:** | They will be with us in America soon enough, and then we won't need photographs to remind us what they look like. |
| **John:** | I have to admit, though, I'm worried about Mother and my siblings. Don't you remember the awful conditions aboard our ship and all the people who got sick when we sailed two years ago? Several people even died. I still have nightmares about it, and it makes me worry about Mother, Cathleen, and Aiden's voyage. |

**Edward:** Of course I remember, Son. I pray that the horrendous conditions we experienced have improved and that our family will enjoy an easier journey. Even if conditions are still poor, I believe the journey is worth the risk for us to be together again.

John: I've also been thinking about our apartment. Will we be able to move into a bigger place after they arrive?

**Edward:** I can't fathom being able to pay for a bigger apartment with our current wages. Every penny of our savings will be spent on tickets for the family's journey to America.

John: But there's barely enough room for two beds here. It's even tinier than our cottage back in Ireland. And just wait until Mother sees all the stairs she'll have to climb to get to the apartment.

**Edward:** I know that we will be cramped in these tight quarters for a while, but you need to trust that our lives will be better when our family is together again. Can't you see your mother's lovely eyes and taste her mouth-watering stew, as we speak?

John: I have heard that there's a storm heading directly toward New York in the coming days. I hope the nasty weather doesn't interfere with their trip.

**Edward:** We must say a prayer that they arrive safely at their destination. I suspect that even with stormy weather, the risk they are taking will be less than if they remain in Ireland.

# Act 3

| | |
|---|---|
| **Cathleen:** | Aiden, have you finally finished packing your belongings? Why is your luggage so incredibly heavy? You understand that you can't take every one of your books, don't you? |
| **Aiden:** | But Mother gave me permission! Anyhow, you're taking all your girly clothing, so why can't I take all my books? |
| **Cathleen:** | Do whatever you desire, but just understand that you'll be the one who will have to carry them. I won't be able to help carry anything, even if you're whining. |
| **Mary:** | Children, are you finally ready? We must arrive at the train station as early as possible to allow plenty of time to get to the port. The tickets indicate that we will be sailing on the SS *Nevada*. |
| **Aiden:** | I'm so excited to finally be leaving! How long do you imagine our journey will be, Mother? |
| **Dylan:** | I hope I'm not interrupting, Mrs. Feeney, but I would like to say farewell to Cathleen. |
| **Mary:** | I'm certain Cathleen wants to say goodbye, too, Dylan. Has your father's condition improved? |
| **Dylan:** | I'm sorry to say that Father's condition has worsened, and Dr. McCreary doesn't know if he'll survive the weekend. |

**Cathleen:** Oh, Dylan, my heart is breaking for you and your family. Please offer my sincere condolences to your mother and siblings. If only I could be here for you during this difficult time, but I'm leaving for my voyage shortly.

**Dylan:** I understand, Cathleen, but promise you will write me a letter the moment you arrive in New York City. I will worry until I receive your correspondence.

**Cathleen:** I will, Dylan, and here is my father's address, so I'll be expecting a letter back. I hope we will see each other again one day, perhaps here in Ireland or maybe in America.

**Dylan:** Regardless of where it is, I sincerely hope that one day we will be reunited. I pray that you and your family have safe travels and are very happy in America.

**Act 4**

**Mary:** My name is Mary Feeney and my children and I are traveling to New York City to be reunited with the rest of our family. Yes, we are all perfectly healthy. Religion? We are Irish Catholic, and no, I most certainly have never been in prison. Yes, we are educated and literate. Goodness, there must be 30 personal questions on this paperwork!

| | |
|---|---|
| Aiden: | This is the largest steamship I've seen in my entire life! I'll bet there will be hundreds, maybe even thousands, of travelers boarding today. Can you believe all of these people are going to New York City? |
| Cathleen: | Obviously, Aiden. But America is a big country, and most of these people will travel on trains to other cities. |
| Aiden: | Mother, that teenager over there told me he had to get a vaccination before he boarded and that it really hurt. Will we need vaccinations, too? Nobody told me that we'd need to get shots to go to the United States. |
| Mary: | If we do, Aiden, then I fully expect you to be brave. A vaccination is not going to prevent us from leaving for America today. |
| Cathleen: | The line is finally moving; let's hurry to find our accommodations! I see several signs for first and second class. Where are our quarters located, Mother? |
| Mary: | I'm afraid we're in neither area; our tickets indicate that we're traveling in steerage. Let's make our way over to that gentleman holding the sign. |
| Aiden: | What does *steerage* mean, Mother? I thought our sleeping quarters would be on the upper decks; I don't understand why they are leading everyone downstairs to the lower deck. Yuck, what's that appalling smell, Mother? |
| Mary: | We'll survive, Aiden, regardless of the conditions. |

| | |
|---|---|
| Cathleen: | It's horrible down here in steerage, Mother. It's filthy and freezing, and the food smells disgusting and rancid. The motion already seems violent, and we have barely left the port. |
| Aiden: | I've already counted seven people getting seasick. It's so horribly crowded—there are practically 200 people down here. And it seems like nearly everyone is speaking different languages. Do you think they'll allow us to go to the upper deck to get fresh air during the voyage? |
| Mary: | I'm not sure, Aiden, but let's try to remain optimistic. Twelve days of discomfort is a small price to pay to have our family together again. |
| Aiden: | I'm happy I brought my books to keep me company. I don't care how long the voyage takes, as long as I have interesting pictures to entertain me. |
| Cathleen: | Do you hear the foghorns? I didn't think I would feel so melancholy about the idea of never seeing Ireland again. |
| Mary: | It's natural to have mixed emotions about leaving the only home you've ever known, Cathleen. Aside from that, I cannot wait to lay my eyes upon your father and brother once again. I have been dreaming of this day for two years now, and that dream will get us through this voyage, no matter how difficult. |

# Act 5

**Dylan:**

*Dear Cathleen,*

*It's been barely three days since your departure, so this letter is likely to arrive in New York City even before you do.*

*I hate to be the bearer of bad news, but unfortunately, Father passed away early this morning before the sun came up. Mother is inconsolable, but I know that it's for the best that he is not suffering any longer. The doctor said there was nothing more they could do for him. He said the same virus has already killed hundreds of people across the province, and it's so serious, it has been labeled an epidemic.*

*I am heartbroken, of course, but I need to stay courageous for mother as we plan for the funeral and burial. We will get by, of course, so please don't worry about us. I hope your family is together once again and that I will be sharing happier news with you in my next correspondence.*

*Sincerely yours, today and always,*

*Dylan*

# Act 6

| | |
|---|---|
| **Edward:** | Hurry, Johnny—we need to leave immediately! The family's steamship is scheduled to arrive this afternoon at Ellis Island. I can't stand the thought of your mother arriving in America without a familiar face to greet her and your siblings. |
| John: | Father, I just finished a grueling 17-hour shift at the railyard. Aren't there a couple minutes available to take a quick bath? I don't want to smell terrible when I hug Mother, Cathleen, and Aiden for the first time in two years. |
| **Edward:** | The next ferry departs in under an hour, so if you really think it's necessary, please hurry. |
| John: | Never mind, I'd rather stink than have them disembark with nobody there to meet them. |
| **Edward:** | Did you prepare your bed so that your brother and sister will be able to rest comfortably when they arrive? Do you remember how exhausted you were after our journey? |
| John: | I'd never been so terribly sick in my entire life. I slept for two days straight. I hope their voyage wasn't as difficult. I've been wondering, Father, why didn't our ship dock at Ellis Island when we arrived in America? |

**Edward:**    The Ellis Island Immigration Station opened several months after we arrived in New York, and thousands of immigrants from all over the world are processed there now. There is Ellis Island off in the distance! Isn't it incredible?

John:    The station certainly is massive. I sincerely hope the disembarking process is more efficient than it was when we arrived. I'll never forget that day—it must have taken nearly six hours to get off that ship. Do you think Mother, Cathleen, and Aiden will like New York City?

**Edward:**    I suspect it will take them some time to get accustomed to how tumultuous and complicated city living is after coming from our quiet village. But I'm hopeful that eventually, they'll enjoy it as much as we do. Of course, I think Ireland will always hold a special place in their hearts, as it does in ours.

John:    Do you really still miss Ireland, Father, even after all the hardships?

**Edward:**    I continue to treasure our distant homeland; however, I have always firmly believed that the only reasonable option was for us to immigrate to America. If poverty or hunger didn't finish us, illness certainly would have. But I dearly hope to see Ireland again in the future. Look, there is the ship!

৯৽৶

**Mary:**    Children, we must get in line immediately or we'll be waiting for hours to disembark. Hurry, Aiden, pack up your books as quickly as you can.

**Aiden:** A sailor told me that there are libraries in New York where you can borrow any book you like. You can even take a book of your choosing home with you.

**Mary:** Ireland had libraries, too, Aiden, but I believe the closest one was in Dublin. Look, there must be thousands of people out here, anxiously awaiting their loved ones. How will we ever locate your father and brother?

**Cathleen:** Do you remember all those questions they asked us before we boarded the ship? I just heard that there will be even more questions once we arrive. And there are physical examinations to make sure we are not carrying any contagious diseases into the country.

**Mary:** Like I keep reminding you, Cathleen, it will all be worth it once our family is reunited.

**Edward:** Johnny, there they are! Our family—have you ever seen anything more extraordinary in your lifetime?

## Song: The Shores of Amerikay

# I Am the Little Irish Boy

## by Henry David Thoreau

I am the little Irish boy
That lives in the shanty
I am four years old today
And shall soon be one and twenty
I shall grow up
And be a great man
And shovel all day
As hard as I can.

Down in the deep cut
Where the men lived
Who made the Railroad.

For supper
I have some potato
And sometimes some bread
And then if it's cold
I go right to bed.

I lie on some straw
Under my father's coat
My mother does not cry
And my father does not scold
For I am a little Irish Boy
And I'm four years old.

# The Shores of Amerikay

## Traditional

I'm bidding farewell to the land of my youth,
And the home I love so well,
And the mountains so grand 'round my own native land,
I'm bidding them all farewell.
With an aching heart I'll bid them adieu,
For tomorrow I'll sail far away,
O'er the raging foam for to seek a home,
On the shores of Amerikay.

It's not for the want of employment I'm going,
It's not for the love of fame,
That fortune bright may shine over me,
And give me a glorious name.
It's not for the want of employment I'm going,
O'er the weary and stormy sea,
But to seek a home for my own true love,
On the shores of Amerikay.

And when I am bidding my last farewell,
The tears like rain will blind,
To think of my friends in my own native land,
And the home I'm leaving behind.
But if I'm to die in a foreign land,
And be buried so far, far away,
No fond mother's tears will be shed o'er my grave,
On the shores of Amerikay.

# Glossary

**contagious**—able to be passed from a person or animal to another by touching

**correspondence**—letters that people write to each other

**disembark**—to leave a ship or airplane

**epidemic**—an occurrence in which a disease spreads very quickly and affects a large number of people

**famine**—an extreme scarcity of food

**immigrate**—to come to a country to live there

**inconsolable**—extremely sad and not able to be comforted

**literate**—able to read and write

**melancholy**—a sad mood or feeling

**quarters**—living accommodations

**recuperating**—returning to normal health or strength after being sick or injured

**steerage**—the section on a passenger ship where passengers who had the cheapest tickets would stay

**tumultuous**—loud, excited, and emotional

**vaccination**—shot administered by a doctor to produce or artificially increase immunity to a particular disease

**wager**—an agreement in which people try to guess what will happen and the person who guesses wrong has to give something (such as money) to the person who guesses right

# R-MAN™

## THE ANNUAL

# 2003

£6.99
UK ONLY

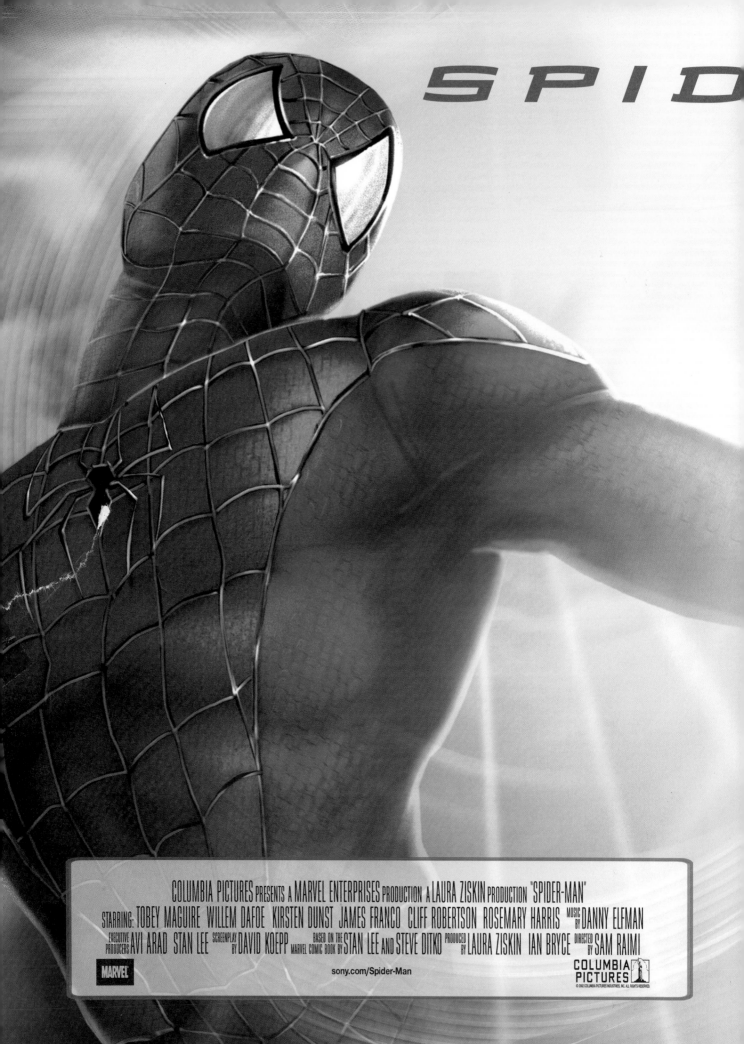

SPID

COLUMBIA PICTURES PRESENTS A MARVEL ENTERPRISES PRODUCTION A LAURA ZISKIN PRODUCTION "Spider-Man"
STARRING: TOBEY MAGUIRE   WILLEM DAFOE   KIRSTEN DUNST   JAMES FRANCO   CLIFF ROBERTSON   ROSEMARY HARRIS   MUSIC BY DANNY ELFMAN
EXECUTIVE PRODUCERS AVI ARAD   STAN LEE   SCREENPLAY BY DAVID KOEPP   BASED ON THE MARVEL COMIC BOOK BY STAN LEE AND STEVE DITKO   PRODUCED BY LAURA ZISKIN   IAN BRYCE   DIRECTED BY SAM RAIMI

MARVEL

sony.com/Spider-Man

COLUMBIA
PICTURES
© 2002 COLUMBIA PICTURES INDUSTRIES, INC. ALL RIGHTS RESERVED.

# ER-MAN™

## CONTENTS

**Written by John Gatehouse**
**Edited by Jane Clempner**
**Designed by Craig Cameron**
**Based on the screenplay by David Koepp**
**Based on the Marvel comic book by Stan Lee and Steve Ditko**
**Photos by Zade Rosenthal, Steve Kahn and Peter Stone**

Spider-Man, the character: TM & © 2002 Marvel Characters, Inc.
Spider-Man, the movie: © 2002 Columbia Pictures Industries, Inc. All rights reserved.
Published in Great Britain in 2002 by Egmont Books Limited,
239 Kensington High Street, London, W8 6SA.
Printed in Italy
ISBN: 0 7498 5609 2

# PETER PARKER
## SPIDER-MAN

Peter Parker, orphaned as a young boy, has been brought up by his doting Aunt May and Uncle Ben.

Now in his teens, Peter has always been a scrawny boy. For this reason, he finds himself bullied at school, especially by Flash Thompson, the school football jerk...er, jock!

But when Peter is bitten by a genetically mutated spider, his life changes forever! He finds that he now has super-strength, can create his own super-strong spider webbing, and possesses a 'spider sense' that warns him of impending danger! He is, in fact,

**...The Amazing Spider-Man!**

SPIDER-MAN

# MARY JANE WATSON

Beautiful, out-going and vibrant, Mary Jane Watson hides a dark secret. She has an abusive father who treats her badly, but she hides her hurt and pain behind her glowing smile.

Mary Jane has always had a soft spot for Peter Parker, but it's not until she, Peter and Harry Osborn move to New York and she begins dating Harry, that her true feelings emerge.

Mary Jane is saved three times from threatening situations by the mysterious figure known only as Spider-Man. She eventually falls deeply in love with Peter ...not realising that Spider-Man and Peter Parker are one and the same!

# AUNT MAY
# AND UNCLE BEN

Orphaned as a very young child, Peter Parker has been raised by his loving Aunt May and Uncle Ben in a suburban neighbourhood in Queens, New York.

Aunt May and Uncle Ben dote on Peter, and have instilled in him a respect for others. When Peter first gains his Spider-Man powers, Uncle Ben notices the sudden change and new-found confidence in his nephew, and gives Peter some sound advice: "With great power comes great responsibility."

Sadly at first, those words fall on deaf ears! When Peter chooses not to stop a robber, and later discovers his uncle has been shot dead in a car-jacking, he tracks down the murderer ...only to discover that the murderer is the robber he could have stopped earlier!

# HARRY OSBORN

Best friend of Peter Parker, Harry is the son of Norman Osborn, millionaire industrialist and owner of the defence company, OsCorp.

Norman Osborn has little time for Harry, and Harry realises that his father would probably sooner have Peter Parker for a son!

When he moves to New York with Peter and Mary Jane Watson, he begins dating Mary Jane in secret, knowing that Peter is in love with her and not wanting to hurt his best friend.

What Harry doesn't know is that Peter himself hides a secret, as does his father. For Peter Parker is really Spider-Man, and his father...the psychopathic Green Goblin!

# FLASH THOMPSON

The school football jock, Flash Thompson is fit, strong, good-looking...and a rotten bully! Popular with the 'in crowd' at school, Flash takes great pleasure in amusing his cronies by picking on others, and his favourite target is Peter Parker!

The high school boyfriend of Mary Jane Watson, Flash feels it his duty to humiliate Peter Parker at every opportunity, and does so with much enjoyment...until the day Peter gains his spider powers, and Flash, to his cost, learns that Peter Parker is no longer anyone's punchbag!

**P**eter Parker never had an easy life.

He had been orphaned as a young child and brought up by his Aunt May and Uncle Ben. As a scrawny kid in spectacles, Peter was always being bullied at school – he never really fit in with people of his own age.

Flash Thompson, the school football jock, took great pleasure in picking on him. And today was going to be no different!

Oversleeping, Peter had almost missed the school bus that was taking his class on a field trip to the Columbia Genetic Research Institute.

He ran after it down the road as it pulled away. If he had known what was to come, how this field trip would change his life forever, he might have decided not to bother!

"Thanks...sorry...sorry... thanks," he gasped, as the bus driver stopped to allow him on board.

Peter walked down the aisle trying in vain to find someone who would let him sit with them. Without warning, one of Flash's friends stuck out his leg and Peter went flying, crashing face down on the floor!

When Flash laughed, his girlfriend, Mary Jane Watson, a girl who lived next door to Peter, gave Flash a withering glare, then stared down at Peter, pity in her eyes.

Without saying a word, an embarrassed Peter sat down in an empty seat and adjusted his glasses, listening to the howls of laughter echoing around the bus...

 At the Columbia Genetic Research

Institute, Peter followed the others off the bus, hanging back until last to keep out of Flash Thompson's way.

He watched as a chauffeur-driven Bentley pulled up. Inside the car was Peter's friend, Harry, and his wealthy father, Norman Osborn, owner of OsCorp.

"Dad, could you drive around the corner?" Harry asked, feeling uncomfortable, as he did most of the time he was in his father's company.

"Why?" asked Norman Osborn, gruffly. "The door's right here."

Harry shook his head. "These are public school kids," he tried in vain to explain. "I'm not showing up in a Bentley."

"What?" his father growled. "You want me to trade in my car because you flunked out of every private school I sent you to? Don't be ashamed of who you are."

"I'm not ashamed. I'm just not..."

"What, Harry?" demanded his father, anger in his voice.

Harry sighed heavily as he got out of the car. "Forget it, Dad." His father would never understand.

Hoping his father would drive away, Harry was dismayed when he got out of the car.

"Won't you be needing this?" snapped Norman Osborn, handing Harry his book bag.

Harry introduced his father to Peter.

"I've heard a lot about you," Norman Osborn said. "Harry tells me you're quite the science whiz."

"Well, I don't know about that," Peter stammered.

"I'm something of a scientist myself, you know," said Norman.

Peter nodded enthusiastically. "I'm familiar with your research."

Just then, the teacher called the class inside the Institute. Peter and Harry said a hurried goodbye to Norman Osborn.

"He doesn't seem so bad," said Peter, as they entered the building.

"Not if you're a genius," Harry muttered darkly. "I think he wants to adopt you!" Then he saw Mary Jane. "Say something," he nudged Peter, knowing Peter's strong feelings towards the girl.

Peter became all flustered. His mouth dried up. He couldn't speak.

The Institute's tour guide took the class around the hi-tech laboratory, which was filled with computer banks and video screens, and a large glass tank, inside of which crawled a number of spiders.

"There are 32,000 species of spider in the world," she told them, as Peter began taking photographs with the camera he had brought along. "The genus Salticus can leap up to forty times it's body length, thanks to a proportionate muscular strength vastly greater than any human being."

The guide droned on about the funnel web spider, one of the deadliest spiders in the world, that could spin a web with strands, equal in tensile strength, in spider terms, to the type of high-tension wire used in bridge building.

And the crab spider, that possessed some kind of 'spider sense' that warned it of approaching danger.

The guide explained that the Institute had mapped out the genetic codes of these spiders. Armed with these DNA blueprints, they had begun inter-species genetic transmutation. The end result – the fifteen super-spiders now kept in the tank.

"There's only fourteen spiders," said Mary Jane, peering into the tank.

Frowning, the guide began to count the spiders but soon gave up and the group moved on. Peter grabbed the chance to ask Mary Jane if he could take her photo.

"I need a shot with a student in it," he explained.

"Sure! Don't make me look ugly," she giggled.

"Impossible," said Peter, shyly, taking photograph after photograph, unaware that a tiny spider, the fifteenth spider that had somehow escaped from the tank, was hanging on a thread directly above him.

Mary Jane wandered back to rejoin the group and the spider began to descend.

Dropping silently, it landed on Peter's right hand, its fangs biting through his skin!

"Ow!" he cried out, shaking his hand in pain.

The spider dropped to the floor and scurried away. Looking at his hand, Peter could see two tiny red marks where the spider had bitten him...

**O**sCorp, a sprawling lab complex hundreds of feet below ground level, was a thriving weapons and technology research centre.

They had recently developed the Individual Personnel Transport, a flying glider that looked like a boogie board, with upturned fins on each side, footholds carved into the wings, and a centre tube jet engine.

They had also designed a lightweight, super tight-fitting electronic suit that allowed the wearer to both operate and control the glider.

But no matter how successful these designs had been, this morning, trouble was brewing for Norman Osborn.

General Slocum, head of a Military Research and Development programme, had paid him a surprise visit, along with The Board of Directors of the company, including Mr Balkan and Mr Fargas.

For five and a half years OsCorp had been contracted to create a super-soldier formula – Human Performance Enhancers – for the United States government. So far, all experiments had failed.

"We tried vapour inhalation with rodent subjects," Doctor Mendel Stromm, head of OsCorp's research unit, explained to the angry general. They stood next to a glass-walled isolation chamber, within which several scientists

worked on a bank of equipment. "They showed an 800 per cent increase in strength."

"Any side effects?" demanded Slocum.

"In one trial, yes..."

Norman Osborn cut him off. "It was an aberration," he said quickly. "All the tests since then have been successful."

Slocum frowned. "What were the side effects?"

"Violence, aggression, and eventually..." said Stromm, "insanity! We need to take the whole line back to formula."

Norman Osborn glared at Stromm. He could have killed him with his bare hands!

"I'll be frank with you," barked General Slocum to Osborn. "I never supported your programme."

Fargas, sitting in his wheelchair, turned to face Osborn. "The General has given the go-ahead to Quest Aerospace to build a prototype of their exoskeleton design. They test in two weeks."

"If your so-called Human Performance Enhancers haven't had a successful human trial by that time," snapped General Slocum, "I will pull your funding and give it to them."

Directors Fargas and Balkan glared at Osborn. "Norman," said Fargas coldly. "We are not going to lose this contract."

Norman Osborn's heart raced. What was he going to do?

Later that day, in his bedroom, Peter Parker was kneeling on the floor, clutching his stomach in pain.

All that afternoon, he had felt violently ill. He was sweating, burning up. The spider's venom coursed through his veins. His body was on fire! The pain was unimaginable!

He had managed to stagger home, and ignoring his Aunt May and Uncle Ben, who were busy preparing dinner, he had dashed to his room, slammed the door, and collapsed on the floor!

"Help!" he now gasped, writhing in agony. He looked at the spot where the spider had bitten him. It was red and swollen.

Cold sweat was running down his face, his body shook uncontrollably. The bedroom began to swim in and out of focus. His eyes rolled up into the back of his head...and Peter Parker passed out!

change, and caught a glimpse of himself in the mirror. He screamed in fright!

His scrawny body was now contoured and muscular. He looked like a champion athlete!

There was a knock on his bedroom door.

"Peter?" called out his worried Aunt May, who had heard the scream. "Are you alright?"

"Fine! I'm fine!" chuckled Peter, flexing his muscles in the mirror. "Just fine!"

"Any better this morning?" asked his Aunt. "Any change?"

Peter looked at himself in the mirror. Then he tossed his glasses into the trash can.

"Change!" he almost hollered. "Yes! Yes! A big change!"

Then he noticed Mary Jane leaving her house next door.

He woke up the next morning, sunlight streaming through his window. Shakily, he got to his feet, yet even as he did so, he knew he felt better. A lot better. Better than he had ever felt in his life!

Then he noticed the time. He was late for school again!

Putting on his glasses, he realised that wearing his glasses made everything look fuzzy, yet without them on he could see clearly. He had perfect vision!

"Weird!" he gasped.

He pulled off his shirt to

Once dressed, Peter went bounding down the stairs, leaping over the banister, landing with acrobatic grace behind his Uncle Ben.

"We thought you were sick," his Uncle Ben was saying.

"I was," said Peter. "I got better."

"Don't forget, we're painting the kitchen today," his Uncle Ben reminded him. "Home right after school."

"Sure thing, Uncle Ben," said Peter, snatching up his backpack and heading out the door, full of energy. "Don't start without me."

He hurried down the road, to catch up with Mary Jane.

"Talk to her... talk to her..." he kept repeating to himself.

But then her friends pulled up in a convertible. Mary Jane got in and the car zoomed away.

With a heavy heart, Peter made his way to catch the school bus. There it was again, pulling away from the bus stop!

Chasing after it, running faster than he ever had, he reached out to pound on the side, to get the driver to stop.

His hand touched a school banner that was pinned on the side of the bus. As the bus accelerated away, Peter realised that his hand was STUCK to the banner.

It ripped off, still stuck on his hand...

**Story continues on page 18**

WORD SEARCH

The words listed below are all associated with Spider-Man.

Can you find them in the word grid? The words can be found forwards, backwards or diagonally.

With a pencil, draw a line through the words you find.

The words to look for are: **AGILITY BALANCE BRAVERY POWERS REFLEXES SPIDER SENSE STAMINA STRENGTH**

| B | R | A | V | E | R | Y | E | P |
| A | S | R | E | W | O | P | H | I |
| L | G | D | N | R | M | T | S | A |
| A | A | I | N | G | G | S | P | N |
| N | S | E | L | N | S | A | I | I |
| C | W | E | E | I | E | M | D | M |
| E | S | R | N | T | T | O | E | A |
| O | T | T | E | S | Z | Y | R | T |
| S | R | E | F | L | E | X | E | S |

# SPIDERS, SPIDERS, EVERYWHERE

**T**he DNA genetically mutated spider that turned puny Peter Parker into Spider-Man isn't the only one to escape from Columbia Genetic Research Institute! Look at this lot! **Eeeek!**

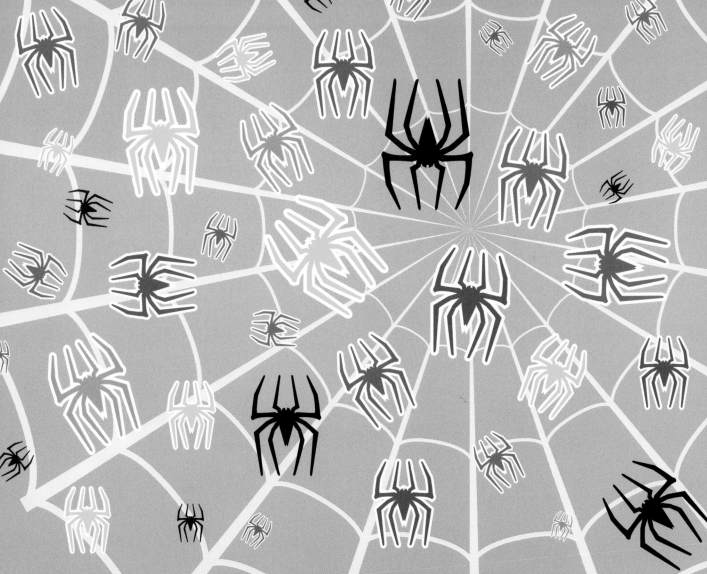

**Can you count how many spiders there are of each colour? Write your answers in the boxes below!**

 8
 5
 6
 9
 7
 10

Answers
There are 9 blue spiders, 6 red spiders, 10 black spiders, 8 yellow spiders, 7 green spiders and 5 orange spiders.

**17**

**L**ater that day, at dinner break, Peter was in the cafeteria eating his meal when he spotted Mary Jane Watson. She was carrying a tray overburdened with food. Suddenly, she slipped on some spilled orange juice, her feet flying out from under her. She was about to crash-land – hard!

Peter's new spider reflexes kicked into high gear and he moved with lightning speed across the cafeteria, catching Mary Jane with one hand, the tray of food with the other.

Mary Jane looked at him. "Wow. Nice reflexes," she said, clearly impressed.

Peter shrugged, freaked out. He couldn't believe he had done it, either.

"No problem," he stammered. Mary Jane waited for more, but nothing came. Peter was too tongue-tied to speak!

"Well, see ya," she said, walking off to sit with Flash Thompson and her friends. But before she did, she looked back over her shoulder at Peter, and smiled.

Peter groaned. He had blown it again.

Dejected, he sat down at a table, all alone. Picking up his fork, he began to eat. In fact, he wolfed down the food! If his Aunt May had seen him, she'd have given Peter a good scolding!

Thirsty, he put down his fork...but it remained stuck to his hand! He tried to pull it free with his other hand, but a long, gooey, web-like strand stretched from his hand to the fork.

A frightened Peter tried to separate the fork from the strand, only for another strand to shoot out of his hand!

This strand flew across to the table next to his own, sticking to a tray of food a girl was eating. Luckily, she was too busy gossiping with her friend to notice.

Shocked, Peter stood up, whipping his arm back, trying to pull free of the strand. But his movement yanked the tray off the table. It flew backwards through the air, the strand finally coming free.

Relieved, Peter turned, and his heart sank! The tray of food had landed all over Flash Thompson!

"Parker?!" bellowed Flash, leaping to his feet. Mary Jane giggled. Horrified, Peter hurried out of the cafeteria...

He stopped in the hallway, beside some lockers. Looking down at his hands, he noticed two almost invisible slits, one on each wrist!

Suddenly, his mind was rocked by the strangest of feelings. Everything slowed down, and it was as if he was seeing outside himself, seeing everything, from all angles, all at once!

And what he saw was Flash Thompson's fist heading, in slow motion, for the back of his head!

As quickly as it turned on, Peter's 'spider sense' turned off again. He whipped around and darted to the side, a split second before Flash's fist flew past his head and smashed into the locker where he had been standing!

Grunting in pain, Flash glared at Peter.

"Think you're pretty funny, don't you, Freak?!"

Mary Jane ran up. "It was an accident!" she cried, knowing what Flash was capable of.

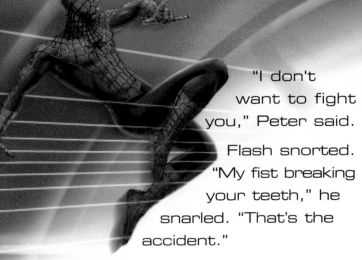

"I don't want to fight you," Peter said.

Flash snorted. "My fist breaking your teeth," he snarled. "That's the accident."

Flash swung at Peter twice with his fists, but each time, Peter evaded them. Then one of Flash's cronies tried to grab him from behind, but sensing the attack, Peter flipped up in the air over him.

Enraged, Flash roared and lunged at Peter! He threw one, two, three, four punches, missing every time as Peter swung his body in a blur of motion, Flash's fists unable to connect!

By this time, a crowd had gathered, including Harry Osborn.

"Harry, please help him," Mary Jane pleaded. Harry stood there, impressed by Peter's actions.

"Which one?" he asked.

Flash lunged at Peter, and Peter, who had grown sick and tired of being Flash's punchbag for all these years, finally threw a punch himself. He struck Flash hard on the chest. Flash went flying down the hall, colliding with a teacher carrying a lunch tray, and slumped to the floor, chocolate pudding running down his face!

"Parker," gasped Flash's disbelieving crony. "You really are a freak!"

Peter looked down at Flash laying on the floor and then to his own hands. Terrified of his new-found strength, he turned on his heels and took off down the hall!

 **T**rying to make some sense of what was happening to him, Peter bunked off school for the rest of the day. He walked along the streets, his mind racing with possibilities.

He turned into an alley, and noticed a beautiful spiderweb that a spider had spun between a dumpster and the alley wall.

Everything slowed in his mind and a cold chill ran up his spine. He remembered the spider bite...surely not? These changes...these new powers... it was too weird!

Making sure he was alone, Peter reached out to touch the wall...and tiny, microscopic hairs leapt out of his pores, clinging tightly to the wall as he touched it.

Slowly, nervously, Peter Parker began to climb up the wall! Incredibly, he didn't fall. He climbed and climbed until he had reached the rooftops.

Remembering the leap he had made earlier, Peter looked over to the rooftop opposite. No human could leap across such a wide gap. He looked down to the streets. He was so high up, he could hardly make out the people below.

Heart thumping, Peter jumped!

He sailed through the air...and landed safely on the next rooftop! He'd made it!!!

Yelling with excitement, Peter leapt from rooftop to rooftop!

This was the most amazing thing that had ever happened to him!

Moments later, he pulled up short. Peter realised that the next gap was too far to leap, even for him.

He looked down at his wrists, seeing the tiny slits. Getting a crazy idea, he pointed his wrist at a taller building across the alley.

He wriggled his wrist, trying to get the goop that had appeared in the cafeteria to come out again. No luck! He made a fist. Nothing! He turned

21

his hand, palm up, extending his fingers, then brought his ring and middle fingers together towards his palm...

**THWIP!** A single strand of webbing shot out of his wrist, straight up. Peter tried again. This time his aim was better. The strand flew across the alley and stuck to the side of the building.

Peter tested the web's strength. It was tough. Very tough. He wrapped his hand around it. Closing his eyes and muttering a prayer, he jumped off the roof!

Peter sailed through the air...straight into the side of the building! **SPLAAT!** He clung there with his hands and feet, his face crushed against the brickwork.

Learning hurt!

That evening, while his Aunt and Uncle were out, Peter saw Mary Jane coming out of her house in a hurry. He could hear her father shouting and raging from inside the house.

He went out to the back yard to take out the trash.

"Hi," he said, embarrassed.

"Were you listening to that?" asked Mary Jane, indicating her house.

"No!" said Peter, rattled. "Yeah! I heard something, but I wasn't listening."

Mary Jane smiled. Peter could be so sweet. And kind.

"So," she asked, "where to after you graduate?"

Peter considered. "I thought I'd go to the city, get a job as a photographer, work my way through college. And you?"

"I'm headed for the city, too. I can't wait to get out of here. I want to...act...on stage. Be an actress."

"Hey, that's great," said Peter, but before he had time to say much more, Flash Thompson arrived in his birthday present – a brand new convertible!

Mary Jane smiled. "Gotta go," she said, before joining Flash in the car.

Peter, watching the car disappear, suddenly felt terribly downcast.

All these special powers he now had, and he still couldn't get the one thing in this world he really wanted... Mary Jane Watson!

Going back inside, he spent the rest of the evening practising how to fire his webs.

Glancing in the newspaper Peter noticed an advert for the local wrestling arena:

# ATTENTION
## AMATEUR WRESTLERS
### THREE THOUSAND DOLLARS
For just three minutes in the ring!
**Colourful Characters a MUST!**

Peter wanted that money. He wanted it so he could afford a car like the one Flash Thompson owned. And he wanted the car to impress Mary Jane Watson!

Night at OsCorp, and in the laboratory Norman Osborn was setting in motion events that would change both his and Peter Parker's lives – forever!

In an isolation tank, Osborn worked furtively with Doctor Stromm, preparing to test the Human Enhancement Performers – on himself!

"Mr Osborn," protested Stromm. "Please, I'm asking

you for the last time, I just need two weeks..."

"Don't be a coward," snapped Osborn. "In two weeks this project, this company, will be dead. Sometimes you have to do things for yourself."

Strapping Osborn to a gurney, Stromm left the tank to operate the control console. With a heavy heart, he flicked a switch.

Inside the tank, a thick, noxious gas rose, creeping over Norman Osborn.

He breathed in...!

Suddenly, his whole body began to convulse!

Stromm hit a button and the gas was sucked back out of the tank. Hurriedly, he re-entered, racing over to the lifeless body of Norman Osborn.

Osborn's eyes popped open. He sat up,

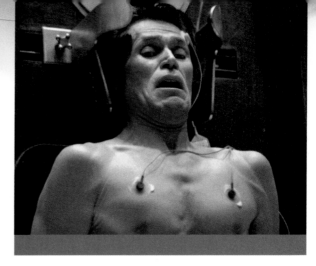

snapping the straps as he did so. He roared in pain!

Stromm tried to restrain him, but Osborn struck out with his arm. Stromm was thrown across the chamber and through the tank's glass wall. The wall exploded in a shower of glass!

Stromm's body crashed against a pillar on the other side of the lab, bones snapping like twigs. He dropped to the floor – DEAD!

Dripping sweat, Osborn leapt out of the tank. He ignored Stromm's body, staring instead at the remote-

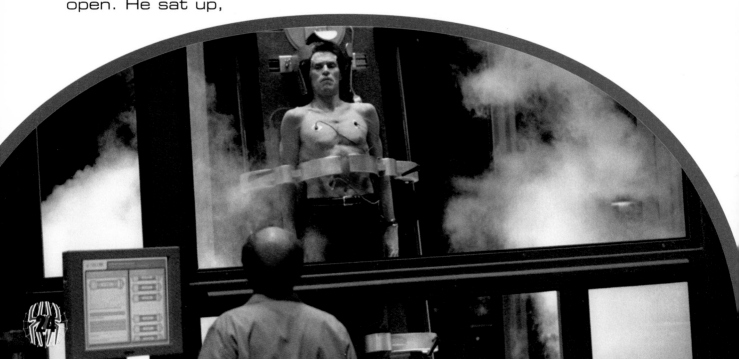

controlled flying platform and body armour.

Throwing back his head, he howled in pain, confusion...and transformation!

 **A** few days later, Uncle Ben drove Peter to the library.

"Thanks for the ride," Peter said, as they pulled up to the curb.

"Hold on a minute," said Uncle Ben. "We need to talk. Your Aunt May and I don't know who you are any more – starting fights in school."

"I didn't start that fight," Peter protested.

Uncle Ben ignored him. "Something new is happening to you, you're changing. When I was your age, I went through exactly the same thing."

"Not exactly," Peter muttered, under his breath.

"Just be careful who you change into. You're feeling this great power...and with great power comes great responsibility."

"Stop worrying about me, okay?" Peter snapped. "Stop lecturing me."

"I know I'm not your father, Peter," Uncle Ben tried to continue, but Peter interrupted him.

"Then stop pretending to be," he said, grabbing his backpack and stepping out of the car.

Watching the car drive away, Peter groaned. He wished he had never said that. Not to loving, caring, Uncle Ben!

**E**vening found Peter at the wrestling arena he'd seen in the newspaper advert.

The arena rang with the deafening roar of the crowd. They were baying for Bone Saw McGraw, the arena's most powerful wrestler, to win his bout against his latest opponent. They were baying for blood!

Peter grimaced as he watched McGraw in the arena, three hundred pounds of pure muscle, taking his opponent apart, piece by piece.

His opponent didn't stand a chance!

Having already signed up for the contest, Peter waited his turn behind a curtain on a ramp that lead to the ring. Butterflies were performing somersaults in his stomach.

His fear grew even more intense as he stepped into the ring and discovered that, to whip up more hysteria from the crowd, he would be fighting Bone Saw McGraw...inside a large, iron cage!

"What am I doing here?" he groaned, after he had been locked inside the cage with the psychotic wrestler!

He was disguised in a baggy, homemade costume, made from old sweatpants, a sweatshirt and a balaclava.

"The Human Spider?" snorted the ring announcer. "That's it? That's the best you've got? Nah, you gotta jazz it up a little."

The curtain parted. It was time for Peter to fight!

**"Let's hear it for the terrifying...the deadly... THE AMAZING!!..."**

The announcer warmly introduced him.

## "SPIDER-MAN!!!"

The crowd went wild with excitement! Screaming taunts and heckles accompanied his long walk to the ring.

Peter was paralysed with fear!

The bell rang, and Bone Saw lunged at him! Peter leapt over his head. Bone Saw crashed into the side of the cage, bounced off, and crumpled to the ground.

He looked up to see 'Spider-Man' clinging to the roof of the cage.

"What do you think you're doing?" the angry wrestler demanded.

"Staying away from you," Peter replied.

Bone Saw leapt at him! Peter somersaulted to the opposite side of the cage.

The crowd went wild! "Yeahhhhhhhh!

Go Spider-Man!" they screamed.

Peter couldn't believe it! They liked him!

A shadow fell on him. Bone Saw grabbed him and pitched him hard against the cage bars. Peter slumped to the ground!

He looked up to see Bone Saw flying down at him, elbow ready to smash into his chest. Flipping up his feet, Peter kicked out, sending an astonished Bone Saw flying across the cage. He slumped to the mat, out cold!

The crowd freaked out!

# SPIDER-MAN!
# SPIDER-MAN!
# SPIDER-MAN!

Under his balaclava, Peter Parker smiled.

But he wasn't smiling, moments later, when the promoter of the wrestling match refused to pay him more than one hundred dollars!

"Check the ad, webhead. It said three grand for three minutes. You pinned him in two."

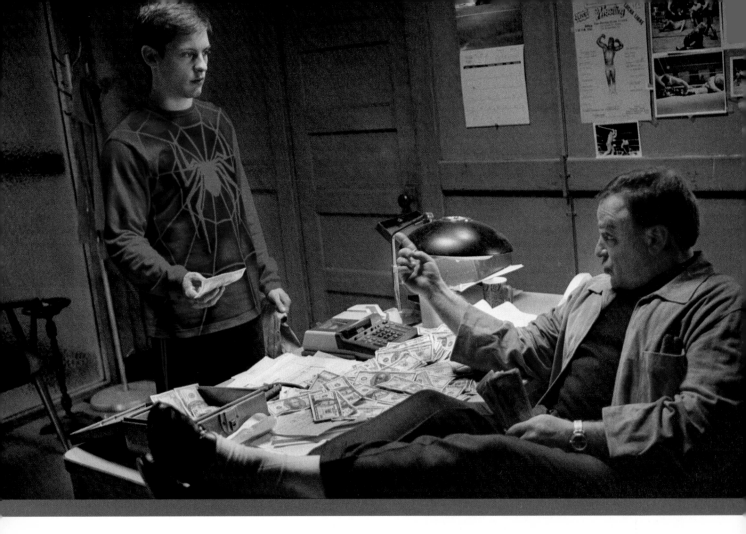

"I need that money!" Peter protested.

The promoter snorted. "I missed the part where that's *my* problem."

Peter, fuming, left the office, passing a squirrelly-looking young man on the way in, the man's hair dyed platinum blonde.

Peter walked to the elevator, waiting for it to arrive. Suddenly, the man re-appeared from the office, clutching a canvas bag full of money!

He raced to the elevator as the doors opened.

"Help! That guy stole the takings," cried the promoter, hurrying out of the office. "He's got my money!"

Peter looked at the thief, running for the elevator. He debated for a moment, then stepped aside. The thief dived into the elevator, hit the button, and the elevator began its descent.

"You could have taken that guy apart!" the promoter raged at Peter. "Now he's gonna get away with my money!"

Peter snorted. "I missed the part where that's *my*

problem," he said, before turning and walking away down the corridor.

**Peter would soon discover, to his cost, that this would be the biggest mistake of his life!**

Fifteen minutes later, Peter, dressed in street clothes again, was outside the public library, waiting for his Uncle Ben to arrive to pick him up.

A police car streaked past, followed by an ambulance, sirens screaming.

Peter's spider sense began tingling. Something was wrong! Taking off, he ran after them, until he came to a street where a large crowd had gathered.

Pushing his way through to the front of the crowd, he stopped, heart racing. There, laying on the sidewalk in a pool of blood...was his Uncle Ben!

"Carjacker," explained a police officer. "He's been shot."

Kneeling, eyes burning with heartfelt tears, Peter cradled his uncle gently in his arms. Uncle Ben opened his eyes and smiled. "Pete," he croaked...and then Uncle Ben died in Peter's arms!

**Story continues on page 36**

# NORMAN OSBORN
## THE GREEN GOBLIN

When millionaire industrialist Norman Osborn, owner of OsCorp, uses his company's untested Human Performance Enhancers on himself, he transforms into the deadly, deranged master of evil – the Green Goblin!

Armed with his explosive pumpkin bombs, the Green Goblin soars through the city on his supersonic Goblin Glider, leaving fear and destruction in his wake!

Discovering that Peter Parker, the boy he has always looked on as a son, is really his arch-enemy, Spider-Man, twists the Green Goblin's already warped mind even further. He attacks the people Peter Parker cares for the most...Aunt May and Mary Jane Watson! When Spider-Man tracks him down, there can only be one outcome to the furious battle – it's a fight to the death!

**Oh, no!** The Green Goblin has genetically engineered a double of himself to fool Spider-Man!

Can you find and circle eight things missing
that could help Spider-Man
tell the difference?

How many words of three letters or more can you make from the word Spider-Man? You might like to ask a friend to help you – or perhaps you could see who can get the most!

Write each word in one of the answer boxes and count up your score at the end!

40

| | |
|---|---|
| spider | dear |
| man | ~~~~ dire |
| men | rain |
| den | rained |
| pit | spire |
| pan | nip |
| pain | pin |
| pen | sea |
| spine | pea |
| mine | ~~dream~~ dream |
| dine | ~~~~ pine |
| die | mine |
| dead | |
| spain | |
| pride | |
| spend | |
| ~~~~ ~~~~ spied | |
| ~~~~ spin | |
| spear | |

**How did you score?**

0-10 – try again!      20-30 – amazing!

10-20 – good effort!  Over 30 – a true hero!

# ALL WEBBED UP

Oops! Spidey's tried catching the Green Goblin with his web-lines, but he's also caught some of his friends! Can you figure out which web-line will lead him to the Green Goblin?

A   B   C   D

**P**eter's grief was interrupted by an urgent call on a police officer's radio.

"They've got the shooter! He's headed south, on Fifth Avenue!"

Peter listened, stony-faced... then he was gone!

He raced down a darkened alley, violently wrenching off his clothes to reveal his costume. He pulled out his mask, slipped it on, and leapt for the side of a building, scurrying up at full speed.

Leaping from rooftop to rooftop, Peter scanned the horizon. Seeing a cluster of police lights screaming down Fifth Avenue, he raised his right arm, releasing a silver strand of web fluid across the street.

He leapt off the roof, swinging over the city, creating one web-line after another, until he was above Fifth Avenue.

Then he saw it! Uncle Ben's car, screeching around a corner, smashing through a row of newspaper stands! Three police cars followed, some distance behind.

Peter dropped from the sky, landing with a heavy thud on the roof of the car.

He punched his fist through the roof, grabbing hold of the carjacker's face!

Gunshots from inside the car erupted through the roof – **BANG! BANG! BANG!** missing Peter by a hairsbreadth! He somersaulted backwards off the roof, landing on top of a truck passing in the next lane.

Seconds later, he had jumped back on to Uncle Ben's car, smashing his fist through the windscreen!

The car swerved, crashing through the gates of a derelict building next to the harbour, screeching at speed towards the entrance.

Realising he would be crushed by the impact, Peter leapt up, out of sight...!

Sweeping searchlights from a police patrol boat shone through the broken windows of the building, illuminating the carjacker as he cowered in a corner.

In the darkness, Peter descended from a web.

The thief turned, shooting wildly with his gun. Peter did an acrobatic leap, landing on the carjacker's arm, sending the gun skittering across the dusty floor.

"This is for the man you killed," snarled Peter, punching the carjacker hard on the jaw and sending him flying backwards! Peter grabbed him, lifting him off his feet.

Another sweep of the police searchlights illuminated his face, and Peter saw him clearly for the first time.

It was the man who had stolen the money from the wrestling arena!

In his heart, Peter Parker realised the ghastly truth: **he had failed to stop the very man who had murdered his uncle!**

The carjacker grabbed his gun from the floor and pulled the trigger...

**CLICK!** It was empty!

The carjacker, terrified, staggered back, tripped...and crashed through a window!

**37**

Peter lunged forward to try and save him – too late!

Screaming, the carjacker smashed into the wooden dock below, and lay there, dead! The money he had stolen fluttered in the air around his broken body...

 **L**ater that night, Peter Parker sat on the roof of a tall building, his heart in shreds.

"Uncle Ben," he whispered, hot tears running down his face. "Oh, god, I'm so sorry..."

**I**nside Bunker 6 of the Quest Aerospace Testing Ground, General Slocum was waiting to be impressed.

He had come to watch the first testing of Badger, Quest's military exoskeleton.

"Our exoskeleton has real firepower, General Slocum," Quest's Project Coordinator was saying. They watched as the test pilot, wearing the exoskeleton, flicked a switch on the suit's control panel and the Badger lifted off the ground.

"Nothing would please me more than to put Norman Osborn out of business," the General admitted.

The Badger rose high into the air. The pilot frowned, a green glow reflecting off his visor.

"What is that?" he blurted out. His eyes grew wider. "Oh, my god! What is that?!!!" he screamed. **"NOOOOOO!"**

The Badger exploded in a massive ball of flame!

Emerging through the fireball was the flying platform from OsCorp, ridden by Norman Osborn, who was disguised in the exoskeleton he himself had created.

Operating the controls with his feet, Osborn released a missile from beneath the platform.

Inside the bunker, General Slocum and the Project Coordinator screamed in fear as they watched the missile head straight towards them!

The next few months were a blur to Peter Parker.

After his Uncle Ben's funeral, he graduated from high school, and, along with Harry Osborn, moved to an apartment in downtown Manhattan, New York, to attend college.

He greatly missed his Aunt May, and Mary Jane Watson. He and Mary Jane had lost touch with each other, and he constantly wondered how she was doing.

Never forgetting the words of his Uncle Ben,

**"With great power comes great responsibility,"**

he had decided to make use of his newfound powers, and dedicate his life to fighting crime.

Wearing his striking red-and-blue costume, and taking the name given to him by the ring announcer at the wrestling ring, Peter Parker became... **Spider-Man!**

Swinging across the city on his spider webs, Spider-Man arrested muggers, thieves, carjackers...in fact, anyone who might harm the innocent!

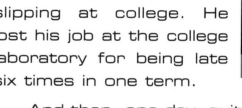

The Daily Bugle, a best-selling newspaper, was up in arms about Spider-Man. Its editor, J. Jonah Jameson, accused him of being both a dangerous vigilante and a public menace!

Jameson would have done anything to get a picture of Spider-Man, knowing that sales of the Bugle would rocket if he appeared on the front page, but not one of his reporters had yet managed to catch him on camera.

"What is he, shy?" he bellowed at deputy editor, Robbie Robertson. "Put an ad on the front page! 'Cash money for a picture of Spider-Man!' He doesn't want to be famous?! Then I'll make him **INFAMOUS!"**

Keeping his Spider-Man identity a secret from the public was hard enough, but spending his free time fighting crime was costing Peter Parker in time and energy.

His grades were slipping at college. He lost his job at the college laboratory for being late six times in one term.

And then, one day, quite by accident, he ran into Mary Jane Watson!

He met her as she was leaving a seedy diner, where she worked as a waitress.

"It's just temporary," she stammered, acutely ashamed. "Few extra dollars."

"That's nothing to be embarrassed about," said Peter. "I've been fired from worse jobs than that."

"Don't tell Harry," Mary Jane pleaded.

Peter stared at her, shell-shocked. "Harry?"

"We've been going out," she explained. "Aren't you guys living together? Didn't he tell you?"

Peter recovered quickly. "Oh, yeah...right. No, I won't tell Harry."

When Mary Jane walked off, Peter stared after her. "Harry and Mary Jane. Wow." And Harry had never told him...!

Peter never mentioned to Harry that he had met Mary Jane. If Harry wanted to keep their relationship a secret, that

was fine by him.

Anyway, Harry had enough trouble with his father, who made weekly visits.

When Peter saw the advert in the Daily Bugle, calling for pictures of Spider-Man, he knew how he could earn money. Lots of money!

Each time Spider-Man foiled a bank robber, or caught a mugger, he took a photograph of himself in action!

He visited the offices of the Daily Bugle, and even though J. Jonah Jameson rubbished Peter's pictures, wanting to pay as little as possible, he still bought them. He knew an exclusive when he saw one!

Soon, Spider-Man was front page news, but not in the way Peter had hoped. Jameson was out to destroy Spider-Man, one way or another!

# SPIDER-MAN:
## HERO OR MENACE?

screamed the headlines, followed the next day by

# NY FEARS
## COSTUMED COWARD

then

# BIG APPLE FEARS SPIDER BITE!

"Why are you so hard on him?" Peter asked Jameson, the next time he visited the Bugle. "He's on the side of the law."

Jameson growled. "He thinks he **IS** the law. There's no place in this society for vigilante justice."

Peter had grown dissatisfied with the bad press Spider-Man was getting.

"I'd like to shoot something other than Spider-Man," he told Jameson.

"No," Jameson snarled. "You just keep doing what you're doing."

Just then, Robbie Robertson came into the office. "J. J., we need someone to cover the World Unity Festival," he said. "Let's send Peter."

Jameson banged his fist on his office table. "World Unity Fesitival? OsCorp sure aims high! Fine, send him." He looked at Peter, holding up a photograph of Spider-Man. **"NOW GET ME MORE PICTURES!"**

At that moment, in the plush offices of OsCorp Corporate Headquarters, Norman Osborn was having an urgent board meeting with his nine fellow directors, including Fargas and Balkan.

Norman Osborn had spent an hour bragging about how successful the company had become.

Balkan and Fargas gave one another an awkward look.

"That's wonderful news, Norman," said Balkan, clearing his throat. "In fact, that's why we're selling the company."

Norman stared at him in disbelief. **"What?!!"**

Balkan continued. "Quest Aerospace is recapitalizing in the wake of the bombing. They're expanding, and they've made an offer we can't refuse."

"But they want you out, Norman," said Fargas. "The deal is off if you come with it. The board expects your resignation in thirty days."

Fury shook through Osborn's body. "You...can't do this to me," he said, scanning the faces of the hostile board members. "I built this company."

"The board is unanimous," Fargas said sharply. "We're announcing the sale right after the World Unity Festival."

Balkan gave a weasel's smile. "You're out, Norman."

Hatred filled Osborn's eyes. "Am I?" he sneered.

The following afternoon, at the World Unity Festival in Times Square, Peter Parker was working his way through the thousands of people who had gathered to enjoy the colourful spectacle.

Huge balloon floats filled the air. A giant, multi-coloured globe stood on a perch in the centre of the Square. Six storeys up, on a viewing stand overlooking the Festival, sat

the OsCorp Board of Directors. Norman Osborn wasn't with them, but his son Harry was, with Mary Jane Watson.

Harry tried to kiss Mary Jane, but she turned her head, only allowing him to kiss her cheek.

Harry glanced down and saw Peter staring up at him. His secret was out!

Peter had seen Mary Jane turn away from Harry's kiss - maybe there was hope

for him yet!

Suddenly, his spider sense went off, jangling furiously!

It was warning Peter of
- **DANGER!**

Looking up, he saw something dart in and out of the clouds, something small, and very, very fast! The crowd cheered, thinking it all part of the Festival!

"Hey," cried Balkan from the reviewing stand. "Is that our glider?"

It was, indeed, and standing upright on it was Norman Osborn, dressed in the exoskeleton. Over his face

43

he wore a grotesque, green demonic mask.

Norman Osborn, his mind having finally snapped, had become the psychotic madman the world would soon be calling **– THE GREEN GOBLIN!**

The Green Goblin sped past the viewing stand and released a bomb from the glider. It exploded against one of the two Hercules statues that were holding the stand aloft! **KA-BOOM!**

Everyone screamed as the stand began to collapse! The OsCorp Board of Directors and Harry were thrown backwards by the blast, Mary Jane forwards! One side of the stand gave way, and Mary Jane went sliding towards the edge!

Below, people ran screaming as chunks of debris rained down on them!

Peter Parker slipped away from the crowd...

Cackling demonically, the Green Goblin banked the Goblin Glider once more, heading back to the crumbling review stand!

He took another pumpkin bomb from his pouch and tossed it on to the stand, at the feet of the nine directors. Exploding in a searing light, it turned the Board of Directors into x-ray images. They screamed – and then they were gone!

The blast caused the stand to separate yet again! Mary Jane was in danger of toppling off!

Rising up behind her on his Goblin Glider, the Green Goblin gave an evil grin. Mary Jane screamed!

The Green Goblin let out a blood-curdling cackle...before he was kicked cleanly off his glider by Spider-Man, swinging through the skies on his web-line!

The Goblin fell, landing on one of the passing floats. He bounced off, twisted in mid-air, and crashed feet first into a large tent below, which broke his fall!

The Goblin Glider zoomed down, puncturing the giant globe and toppling it off it's perch!

Spider-Man, clinging to the side of a building, looked up to Mary Jane, who was holding on desperately to the crumbling stand, about to fall to her death, and then down at the globe, toppling toward the street, about to crush everything in its path!

Directly in front of the globe, frozen with fear, was a little boy!

Without hesitation, Spider-Man fired a web-line at a billboard atop a nearby building. He swung in a huge arc, sweeping up the child, just as the globe crashed to the ground.

Spider-Man lowered the boy safely to the street. He was about to return to save Mary Jane when he saw the Green Goblin mercilessly attacking a group of policemen, hurling them into the air!

Spider-Man somersaulted towards him, landing in front of the Green Goblin!

**BAMM!** He punched the Green Goblin – hard! But the Goblin caught his punch, smiled, and delivered one of his own that sent Spider-Man sailing through the air.

The Green Goblin touched something on his wrist and a moment later his Goblin Glider came whizzing down!

Leaping aboard, the Green Goblin took off into the sky. He banked and small machine guns appeared on the Glider's tips. The Green Goblin raked the street where Spider-Man was standing with machine gun fire! **RAT-A-TAT-TAT!**

Spider-Man leapt out of the way, just in time! Then he saw Mary Jane, about to fall to her death!

Leaping from float to float, Spider-Man had almost reached her when the Green Goblin swooped, grabbing Spider-Man in an unbreakable bear hug, driving him into the building above the balcony! Spider-Man plummeted...and crashed to the floor of the stand, the impact sending Mary Jane rolling to the very edge!

Rising out of nowhere, the Green Goblin appeared, hovering right over them!

Spider-Man shot a web, right into the Green Goblin's face, obscuring his vision, then reached up into the glider and pulled out a handful of wiring from underneath the wing!

The glider, losing control, took off into the skies!

Just then, the building ledge gave way, and Mary Jane fell, screaming!

Spider-Man dived down after her, trailing a web behind him. He caught her just short of the street, the web went taut, and they were pulled back up just as the stand collapsed on to the pavement! **SMAAASSSH!**

Six storeys up, in the room he had been blasted backwards into, Harry awoke to see Spider-Man swinging away, Mary Jane in his arms.

"Who are you?" Mary Jane asked, as they swung across the city, from web to web.

Beneath his mask, Peter Parker smiled. "Your friendly neighbourhood Spider-Man."

Dropping Mary Jane off on the rooftop gardens of a tall building, Spider-Man leapt off the edge, swinging away through the air.

Mary Jane stared at him as he disappeared from sight. "Wow," she gasped.

**Story continues on page 52**

# CAUGHT ON CAMERA

Spider-Man's taken a picture of himself for the Daily Bugle! Can you copy the picture into the blank grid, and then colour it in?

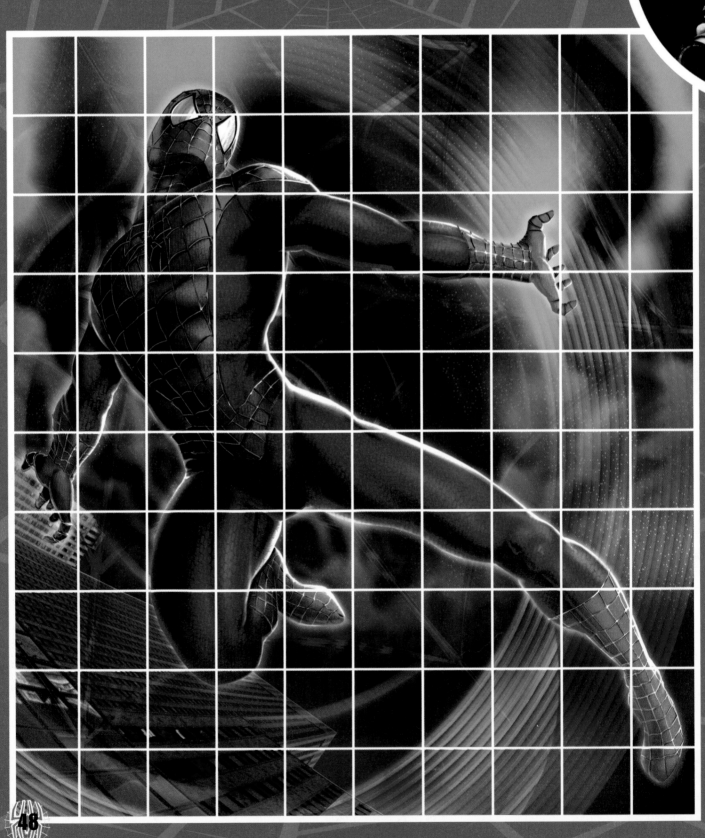

48

You never know – cranky old J. Jonah Jameson might be so impressed, he'll buy it!

# Spider Bytes

## ARACHNO-FACT-O

- All spiders are carnivorous.

- Relatively few spiders bite people because they are not able to pierce the skin with their fangs.

- The commonly called Daddy Long-legs (Order Opiliones, Family Phalangiidae) although sometimes thought to be a spider, is not a spider at all.

- Tarantulas (Order Araneae, Family Theraphosidae) are the largest spiders. Male tarantulas live only a few years but in captivity a female can live for 35 years.

**Banded-legged Golden Orb Web Spider**

Spiders produce sticky threads, or silk, from special glands on their bottoms. Some, such as the Orb Web Spider, use it to build see-through webs, to trap flying insects. Spiders can also use their silk as a lasso, to build nests for their eggs, and even to fly!

The tensility of a spider's web is so strong that the spider would have to be 50,000 times it's size to break the web!

- A protein found in tarantula venom has been shown to prevent atrial fibrillation, a condition marked by irregular heartbeats.

# DID YOU KNOW?

(Source: Explorit Science Center)

- Spiders are believed to have existed for more than 300 million years.

- Spiders secrete oil from their feet, which is why they don't stick to the web. [Source: Fun Facts]

- Arachnophobia is the fear of spiders. [Source: The Phobia List ]

- There are about 35,000 named species of spiders worldwide although it is believed that there are many more still to be identified and named.

- Spiders have lungs. There are two sorts of lungs, neither of which is like a human lung. Some spiders have book lungs (a stack of soft plates) or tracheae (breathing tubes). There appears to be no active, muscular breathing mechanism. Air seems to pass in and out of the book lung or the tracheae in a passive manner.

## Jumping Spiders
### (Order Araneae, Family Salticidae)

**Scanning electron micrograph of the Zebra Spider.**

Jumping spiders are known for their spectacular leaps of up to forty times their body length.

The Zebra Spider is one of the jumping spiders and is so named because of its distinctive black and white colouring. They are common throughout Britain and are found on walls and paths. They hunt their prey by stalking and then jumping on it.

- Most spiders have eight simple eyes. [Insects on the other hand have large, compound eyes.] The two main eyes of a spider each have a simple lens, and a retina made up of light sensitive cells whose surfaces point toward the light as it enters the eye. The secondary eyes also have a lens but the light sensitive cells of these eyes point away from the light as do the similar cells in a human eye.

- Not all spiders spin webs. However, spiders that do not spin webs do produce silk. Some live in burrows, which they line with the silk from their silk glands. Young spiders ride the wind on long silk threads in a process that we call 'ballooning'.

Photographs by Stuart Westmorland, David Burder and Walter Bibikow. Courtesy of Getty Images

Once Harry knew that Mary Jane was safe, he owned up to Peter.

"I know I should have told you about us," he stammered, as they talked in their apartment. "You have to understand, I'm crazy about her. I always knew you wanted her for yourself, but you never made a move."

Peter nodded, sadness in his eyes. "I guess I didn't."

Quickly changing the subject, Harry asked, "What was that thing that killed those people?"

"I don't know," said Peter, quiet determination in his voice. "But somebody has to stop it."

The next morning, Norman Osborn was staring in disbelief at the headlines of the Daily Bugle:

# SPIDER-MAN AND GREEN GOBLIN TERRORIZE CITY!
## OSCORP BOARD MEMBERS KILLED!

Osborn couldn't take it in. How could it have happened? And just who was this Green Goblin?

"Stop pretending, Norman."

Osborn spun round at the sound of the other-worldly voice. "Who said that?" he demanded, looking around the empty room, cold sweat running down his spine. "Who are you?"

The voice echoed inside his head. It seemed to be coming from the mirror. But when he looked, all he saw was his own reflection.

"Did you think it was all coincidence?" the cruel voice continued. "So many good things ...all happening for you...all for you, Norman."

Osborn looked down at the newspaper. "The board members! **YOU** killed them?!"

The voice cackled. "**WE** killed them..."

Osborn's heart lurched as the truth sank in. "Oh, god! Oh, god!" he cried.

The Green Goblin's face appeared in the mirror, reflected over Norman's own.

"Stop whining..." snapped the Green Goblin. "**YOU** are now in full control of OsCorp."

Osborn collapsed in a chair. He smiled. "I suppose the damage has been done."

"There's only one person

who could stop us," the Green Goblin told him.

"Or..." considered Osborn, "be our greatest ally."

"Exactly!" the Green Goblin cackled. "We need to have a chat with you-know-who."

"But how will we find him?" demanded Osborn. And then his eyes dropped to the newspaper, and the picture of Spider-Man and the Green Goblin on the front page of the Daily Bugle...

**L**ater that day, Peter Parker was in the reception room of the Daily Bugle when he heard a loud **SMASH!** Spinning round, he saw the window of J. Jonah Jameson's office explode inwards in a shower of glass!

In swooped the Green Goblin on his Goblin Glider. He grabbed J. Jonah Jameson by the throat, lifting

him off the ground!

"Who's the photographer who takes the pictures of Spider-Man?" the Green Goblin demanded. "Where is he?"

Peter quickly ducked into the hallway...

"Hey," said Spider-Man, moments later, hanging upside down outside the shattered window of Jameson's office. "I wear the tights in this town."

"I knew it!" gasped Jameson, as the Green Goblin dropped him to the floor. "You and Spider-Man are in this together!"

Without speaking, the Green Goblin raised his gloved hand, and sprayed knockout gas directly into Spider-Man's face! Everything went black...!

**S**pider-Man woke to find himself on the roof of a building, the Green Goblin leering over him.

**T**he following day, Spider-Man was in action again. As he was swinging across the city, he heard the loud wailing of fire engines close by.

Arriving on the scene, Spider-Man could see an apartment building, burning fiercely! Realising a baby was trapped inside, he leapt through an open window, into the fire. The crowd of onlookers held their breath. There was a loud creaking noise as the roof started to collapse!

Then Spider-Man reappeared, just before the room exploded in a huge fireball! He was cradling

"Relax," said the Green Goblin. "My hallucigen gas has slowed your central nervous system to a crawl."

Spider-Man tried to rise, but his body wouldn't move!

"Imagine," the Green Goblin continued, "what we could accomplish together." He paused. "**OR**...what we could destroy! Causing the deaths of countless innocents in selfish battle, again and again...until we are both dead."

He summoned his Goblin Glider and leapt aboard.

"Think about it, hero," he finished, cackling demonically before flying off into the night...

the baby in his arm.

But Spider-Man had no time for thanks. A woman screamed from inside the building. Someone was still trapped!

With the fire now raging out of control, Spider-Man didn't think twice! Firing a web-line, he swung back into the building.

In a smoke-filled room, he saw what appeared to be an old woman, draped in a shawl.

The 'old woman' let the shawl fall to the floor.

"Goblin! **YOU?**" gasped Spider-Man in horror. "You started this fire?!"

The Green Goblin cackled. "You're pathetically predictable. Like a moth to a flame," he sneered. "What about my generous proposal? Are you in, or are you out?"

"It's you who's out, Gobby," Spider-Man snapped, preparing to attack. "Out of your mind!"

The Green Goblin reacted first, hurling a razor-sharp bat-shaped weapon, which sunk into Spider-Man's arm!

"**Ahhh!**" he cried, looking down at the deep gash, oozing blood.

Just then, the roof of the building began to collapse, trapping the Green Goblin inside, and giving Spider-Man the chance to escape.

 **A**rriving back at his apartment, his arm still dripping blood, Spider-Man sneaked into his room through the window, only to hear voices downstairs.

It was Harry talking to Mary Jane, Aunt May...and Norman

Osborn! They had all arrived to enjoy a Thanksgiving meal together.

Spider-Man quickly grabbed some clothes and took off out of the window again.

Moments later, Peter Parker opened the front door of the apartment, apologising for being late.

"Peter," cried Aunt May, seeing blood oozing from his shirt sleeve. "You're bleeding!"

She pushed up his sleeve, revealing a diagonal slash in his arm.

"Yeah," said Peter, quickly. "I stepped off the curb and got clipped by a bike messenger."

Norman Osborn stared intently at the wound.

"You'll have to excuse me," he said quickly. "I've got to go."

**N**orman Osborn left the party, his mind whirling. The truth began to dawn on him. He had seen that wound before. But now it was on a human arm.

**Peter Parker was none other than Spider-Man!**

Norman Osborn lay huddled on the floor of his apartment, cowering in a pool of light at the end of the hall. He was clutching the Green Goblin's mask in his hands, talking to it.

"This changes everything..." the Green Goblin hissed in his mind. "Spider-Man is all but invincible...but Parker...Parker is flesh and blood...we can destroy him..."

Norman Osborn wept. "What do I do?"

"Make him suffer...make him wish he were dead...and then...grant him his wish!"

**"TELL ME HOW!"** begged Osborn.

"The heart, Osborn," cackled the Green Goblin. "First we attack his heart."

That same night, all alone in her house, frail Aunt May had a visit...from the Green Goblin!

Peter raced down the hospital corridor, heart thumping in fear and pain. He lurched into a private room. Aunt May lay in a hospital bed, wired up to a heart machine.

Doctors and nurses swarmed around her bruised and battered body.

"Aunt May!" cried Peter. "What happened? Is she going to be okay?!"

"Sir, please!" said a nurse. "Let the doctors work!"

"Eyes...those horrible yellow eyes!" moaned Aunt May.

Peter realised who she meant.

"The Goblin..." he whispered to himself. "He knows...oh, god, he knows who I am..."

Peter was still at Aunt May's bedside the following morning when Mary Jane turned up.

"Is she going to be okay?" she asked.

Peter smiled wanly. "We think so. She finally woke up this morning. Thanks for coming."

Mary Jane sat next to Peter. She took his hand in hers, staring deeply into his eyes.

Harry Osborn, arriving to visit Aunt May, stopped in the doorway. He saw the way Mary Jane looked at Peter. He turned and left.

That night he told his father what he had seen.

"You were right about Mary Jane," he said. "She's in love with Peter. And there's no one Peter cares more about."

Norman Osborn's eyes lit up. No one Peter Parker...Spider-Man...cares more about...!

 **M**ary Jane had already left when Aunt May woke. Peter was still smiling at the thought of the girl he loved.

"Tell me, Peter," Aunt May said, reading his thoughts. "Would it be so dangerous to let Mary Jane know how much you care?"

Peter's smile faded. "So dangerous?"

"Everyone else knows how much you care for her."

"Everyone knows... everyone..."

In the hospital corridor, Peter desperately tried to phone Mary Jane. Her phone rang...and rang...and rang...

"Answer the phone, answer it!" he cried, fear gripping him.

There was a click on the other end.

"Oh, great, you're there," he said, relieved. He had been worrying about nothing, after all. "Hello?"

No answer.
Then a sound.
No...a cackle!
The cackle grew louder.
Then the Green Goblin spoke.

"Can Spider-Man come out to play?"

**M**ary Jane Watson regained consciousness. She pulled herself to her feet, the night wind whipping at her face. Where was she?

She took a step backwards,

then stopped, suddenly, windmilling her arms for balance. Looking down, she gasped in terror at the sight of the roadway of a bridge...hundreds of metres below her!

The Green Goblin appeared, flying through the sky on the Goblin Glider, heading for the tram station next to the bridge.

Cackling with glee, he launched a rocket from the glider into the tram station! The tram station was obliterated in a massive fireball!

### KAA-BOOOOM!

From across the city, Spider-Man heard the explosion.

A tram filled with children and adults had no time to stop. Cables were snapped in the blast, and now the tram, suspended several hundred metres above the river, suddenly dropped!

Spider-Man swung across the city at full speed, and leapt on to the bridge to try and save the people.

Then, strangely, the Green Goblin swooped down, grabbing a cable, stopping the tram's fall! He landed at the top of the bridge tower, holding aloft the tram in one hand...and Mary Jane in the other!

"Make your choice, Spider-Man!" said the Green Goblin. "Let die the woman you love...or suffer the little children."

Spider-Man was momentarily paralysed, torn in half.

"This is why only fools are heroes," the Green Goblin cackled. With that, he let go of Mary Jane on one side of the tower,

and the tram on the other, sending them all to their deaths, hundreds of metres below!

Spider-Man watched in horror, terrified screams assaulting his ears, as the tram fell to the left, Mary Jane to the right! He ran along the bridge and leapt, catching Mary Jane in mid-air!

He shot a web to the undercarriage of the bridge, swinging underneath. Releasing his web, he grabbed the cable of the tram. He and Mary Jane were pulled down by the weight of the tram towards the river below!

Using his free hand he shot out another web to the undercarriage of the bridge, stopping the tram's fall! He was now being stretched apart, one hand holding on to the cable, the other the web!

"The cable to the tram," he grunted to Mary Jane. "Climb down."

Mary Jane, shaking with fear, quickly did as she was told.

The Green Goblin, cackling madly, zoomed in on his glider, punching Spider-Man hard on the jaw! **WHAAACCK!**

Again he attacked, and Spider-Man dropped the cable!

The tram and Mary Jane plunged towards the river!

Spider-Man dangled from his web, grasping for the cable snaking past him. The cable went taut, and Mary Jane was thrown off, landing hard on the roof of the tram!

The Green Goblin raced towards Spider-Man for the killing blow!

Suddenly, a chunk of masonry struck him hard on the side of the head! On the bridge above, bystanders were hurling everything they could at him!

The Green Goblin zoomed off to avoid the raining debris, allowing Spider-Man to safely lower the tram onto a barge.

**Mary Jane and the people in the tram were saved!**

But before a desperately weakened Spider-Man could recover, a rope wrapped around his waist. He was jerked up into the air by the Green Goblin!

Mary Jane watched in horror as Spider-Man was dragged away into the night sky...

**D**ropped from a great height by the Green Goblin, Spider-Man crashed through the roof of an abandoned derelict hospital.

Blood oozing from gaping wounds, he lay on his back, defenceless. The Green Goblin swooped into the building, hovering over him. He pulled a trident from the Goblin Glider, bringing it down towards Spider-Man's chest!

At the last moment, Spider-Man snatched the trident! His strength returning, with his free hand he grabbed the Green Goblin, and punched him hard! The Green Goblin smashed into another wall! Spider-Man hit him again...and again! And again!

"Please..." begged the Green

Goblin, and to save himself, he pulled off his mask!

Spider-Man recoiled in shock! The Green Goblin was none other than his friend...Norman Osborn!

"Can't be..." gasped Spider-Man in disbelief. "You're a monster. You killed those people on the balcony. You tried to kill Aunt May. You tried to kill Mary Jane."

"**IT** killed. The Goblin killed," whined Osborn. "I had nothing to do with it." Without Spider-Man noticing, he touched a control pad on his gloved wrist.

The Goblin Glider rose up behind Spider-Man.

"God speed, Spider-Man," the Green Goblin cackled.

Spider-Man's spider sense kicked in, just as a spear rotated into position on the front of the Goblin Glider. The Glider zoomed across the room, straight for Spider-Man's back!

Spider-Man flipped up into the air, over the glider, and the Green Goblin's own glider rocketed straight through him, the spear pinning his body to the wall! **THUNNK!**

The Green Goblin...
was **dead!**

**62**

**T**o save Harry from learning the dreadful truth about his father, Spider-Man took Norman Osborn's body back to his apartment, and laid him out on a sofa. Unfortunately, Harry came in at that moment, and thought that Spider-Man had killed his father!

At his father's funeral, he swore that Spider-Man would pay!

Mary Jane told Peter how much she loved him. But Peter was in an impossible situation. If anyone else found out that he was really Spider-Man, her life could be put in danger again.

Neither could he give up being Spider-Man, not even for true love.

He realised the truth: it's hard to be a saint in the city.

The words of his Uncle Ben echoed in his ears: "With great power comes great responsibility."

Peter understood now, and his choice was clear.

**He was Spider-Man, and always would be.**

He swung away, shimmering into the glass and stone canyons of the city – a true hero.

**The End**

The Green Goblin has kidnapped Mary Jane Watson – and only Spider-Man can save her! Can you find the route through the spider webs to rescue her?

Watch out for the pumpkin bombs!

Start

Finish

# ARE YOU A SPIDEY FAN OR FOE?

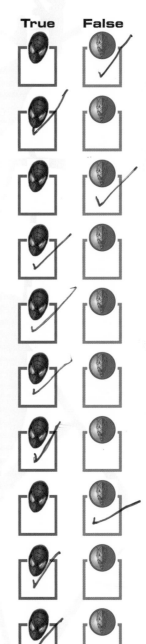

Just how well do you know Spider-Man? Take our true or false test and find out for yourself! Then check the answers at the bottom of the page and add up your score to see how well you did!

|  | True | False |
|---|---|---|
| **1) SPIDER-MAN'S NICKNAME IS SPIKEY** | | ✓ |
| **2) THE DAILY BUGLE IS PUBLISHED IN NEW YORK** | ✓ | |
| **3) THE GREEN GOBLIN'S WEAPONS ARE PUMPKIN PIES** | | ✓ |
| **4) FLASH THOMPSON USED TO BULLY PETER PARKER** | ✓ | |
| **5) AUNT MAY HELPED BRING PETER UP** | ✓ | |
| **6) SPIDER-MAN'S REAL IDENTITY IS PETER PARKER** | ✓ | |
| **7) THE DAILY BUGLE'S EDITOR IS J. JONAH JAMESON** | ✓ | |
| **8) NORMAN OSBORN IS HARRY OSBORN'S SON** | | ✓ |
| **9) SPIDER-MAN CAN CRAWL UP THE SIDES OF BUILDINGS** | ✓ | |
| **10) PETER PARKER'S IN LOVE WITH MARY JANE WATSON** | ✓ | |

**I scored**